Rude Rabbit

BURP!

With thanks to librarians everywhere,
who often come across
Rude Rabbits.

First published in hardback in Great Britain by HarperCollins Publishers Ltd in 2000
First published in paperback by Collins Picture Books in 2001

3 5 7 9 10 8 6 4 2
ISBN: 0-00-664722-7

The HarperCollins website address is: www.fireandwater.com

Printed and bound in Singapore by Imago

Rude Rabbit

Colin and Jacqui Hawkins

An imprint of HarperCollinsPublishers

This is Rude Rabbit.

Rude Rabbit was very rude.
He would gobble and slurp his
food and then loudly BURP!
"Where are your manners?"
asked Greedy Goat.

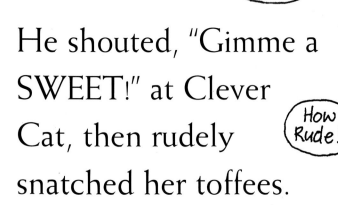

"Up my JUMPER!"
laughed Rude
Rabbit, rudely.

He shouted, "Gimme a
SWEET!" at Clever
Cat, then rudely
snatched her toffees.

Then he pulled rude faces at Mr Bun the Baker and stuck his tongue out at him.

He even shouted, "Oi! FISH FACE!" at Mr Flipper the Fishmonger. Rude Rabbit was so rude!

"HEE! HEE! HEE! You look silly," laughed Rude Rabbit, pointing at Mrs Posh Pig's new hat. "HEE! HEE! What daft glasses you've got," laughed Rude Rabbit at Daft Dog. "All the better to see how rude you are," said Daft Dog as he went on his way to the library.

Whenever Rude Rabbit was in a hurry he never said "Excuse me!" He just pushed and shoved and trod on everyone's toes and shouted, "Get out of my WAY!" No one liked Rude Rabbit, but he was so busy being the rudest rabbit in the world that he didn't notice. Until, one day...

...he saw Honey Bunny. She was the most beautiful rabbit Rude Rabbit had ever seen. He instantly fell head over ears in love with her. "HEY! Honey Bun! Gimme a kiss!" shouted Rude Rabbit rudely. But Honey Bunny just stuck her pretty pink nose in the air and skipped off.

The next day Honey Bunny was out shopping when Rude Rabbit rudely hopped out of a taxi right in front of her.

"HEY! Honey Bun! Gimme a big kiss!" yelled Rude Rabbit, and rudely shoved a big bunch of flowers under her nose.

"NO! Go away." said Honey Bunny, and threw the flowers in the air.

Later Honey Bunny was relaxing in *The Shear Delight Beauty Salon* when the door burst open.
"HEY! Honey Bun! Gimme a kiss!" shouted Rude Rabbit and he rudely pushed a large box of chocolates into her paws.
"NO! NO! You're the rudest rabbit in the world," said Honey Bunny. "Chocolates make me sick – and so do YOU!"

Rude Rabbit was so
shocked that he burst
into tears. "Boo hoo!
What can I do...?"
he wailed.

"No one likes a rude
rabbit," said Daft Dog. "You've got to stop being
so rude. Come with me," and he took Rude
Rabbit off to the library. "Read this,
Rude Rabbit," said Daft Dog.
"The Big Book of Better Manners,"
read Rude Rabbit.
"It's just what you need,"
laughed Daft Dog.

With *The Big Book of Better Manners* Rude Rabbit soon learnt how not to be rude.

Before long Rude Rabbit didn't push and shove any more.

He learnt how to say "please", "thank you" and "after you".

He ate his food properly without slurping or burping, and he stopped pulling rude faces and shouting rude names.

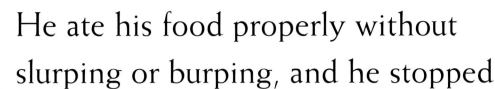

Wow, what a wicked hat!

Oh, thank you, Rude Rabbit!

Everyone thought Rude Rabbit was so much nicer now, even Honey Bunny said...

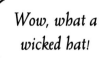

..."You're so polite now, Rude Rabbit." "Everyone should have good manners," said Rude Rabbit. "And I'm just the rabbit to show them."

So he set up *The Rude Rabbit Rudeness Roadshow.* "Rid yourself of rudeness," he said. "Learn in a night to be polite." Everyone laughed and cheered. From then on Rude Rabbit was the politest of rabbits...

...except, of course,
when he forgot his manners!